Stinky Stern Forever

MICHELLE EDWARDS

Harcourt, Inc.

Orlando Austin New York San Diego Toronto London

A big best-in-Frogtown thank-you to
Mrs. Garcia's second-grade class
at Jackson Magnet, for all their help

Requests for permission to make copies of any part of the work should be
mailed to the following address: Permissions Department,
Harcourt, Inc., 6277 Sea Harbor Drive, Orlando, Florida 32887-6777.

www.HarcourtBooks.com

Library of Congress Cataloging-in-Publication Data
Edwards, Michelle.
Stinky Stern forever/Michelle Edwards.
p. cm.
"A Jackson friends book."
Summary: Pa Lia and her classmates share memories
of Stinky Stern, the second-grade bully.
[1. Bullies—Fiction. 2. Death—Fiction. 3. Schools—Fiction.] I. Title.
PZ7.E262St 2005
[Fic]—dc22 2004003141
ISBN 0-15-216389-1

C E G H F D B

Manufactured in China

The illustrations in this book were drawn with a Wacom Pen,
sketched first in Microsoft Paint and then finished in Adobe Photoshop.
The display type was set in Worcester Round Medium.
The text type was set in Sabon.
Manufactured by South China Printing Company, Ltd., China
This book was printed on Japanese matte paper.
Production supervision by Pascha Gerlinger
Designed by Michelle Edwards and Lydia D'moch
Expert technical assistance from Shane Sizer

To kids and stinkers everywhere,
wear your helmets when you ride your bikes.

And always stop, look, and listen
before you cross the street.

Contents

Snowflakes

Pa Lia Vang yawned. It was nearly the end of the school day at Jackson Magnet. Mrs. Fennessey had promised to let the class do a project. Pa Lia hoped it would be something fun.

"Today we will make snowflakes," announced Mrs. Fennessey. "We will decorate our room with them."

Pa Lia sat up straight. She wasn't tired anymore. She loved art projects.

Mrs. Fennessey showed the class how to fold and cut paper into lacy snowflakes.

"You can work by yourself or in groups," she told them.

Howie

Calliope

Pa Lia got three sheets of paper and three scissors. She gave paper and scissors to her two best friends, Howie and Calliope. They all sat in the same row by the window.

Pa Lia was an excellent cutter. She cut and folded and sewed shapes all the time with her grandma to make *paj ntaub,* "story cloths." She finished her snowflake quickly.

"Beautiful," said Calliope.

"Super," said Howie. "Can you help us with ours?"

Pa Lia carefully put her snowflake on her desk. She showed Howie and Calliope how to make a sharp fold. She taught them her grandma's trick of little cuts and turns.

"Great," said Howie.

"Let's hang our snowflakes together," said Calliope.

Pa Lia went back to her desk. There was a big ugly glob of glue right in the middle of her terrific snowflake.

"Snowflake a little sticky, four-eyes? Heh, heh, heh," said Stinky Stern, the enemy of the second grade.

I'm not going to let him ruin my snowflake, thought Pa Lia.

She quickly cut some spirals and triangles and an eight-pointed star. She made a Hmong pattern with the shapes and covered the ugly glue spot.

Pa Lia hung her even more terrific snowflake where Stinky Stern had to see it. Howie and Calliope hung their snowflakes next to hers.

"Heh, heh, heh," Pa Lia chuckled.

The Accident

It happened on Court Street, right after the buses left. Pa Lia and her big brother, Tou Ger, were on their way home.

Pa Lia watched Stinky Stern run across the street. He wasn't even looking. *Running home to think of more mean things to do.*

Pa Lia saw a lady driving by in a white van.

She heard brakes screech. She saw the white van hit Stinky. She leaned close to Tou Ger.

Cars stopped. The lady jumped out of her white van. Someone shouted to call 911.

"Pa Lia, let's go," said Tou Ger. His voice sounded like it was coming from far away.

Pa Lia couldn't move.

The lady from the white van covered Stinky with a plaid blanket. Mr. Scott, the principal, and Mrs. Fennessey came running out of school. Pa Lia saw Mrs. Fennessey kneel down next to Stinky. She could hear her singing to him.

Pa Lia squeezed her eyes shut. The sound of sirens blared in her ears. She opened her eyes. She saw the paramedics putting Stinky on a stretcher and loading him into the ambulance.

Will Stinky be okay? He is so quiet. So still.

The ambulance sped away with its lights flashing and its sirens blasting.

"I know that boy," said Pa Lia. She was crying. "He's in my class."

Tou Ger hugged Pa Lia. He was wearing a puffy down jacket. He was soft and warm to hug.

"We better go or Mom will worry," he said. They were both shaking now.

Pa Lia reached for Tou Ger's hand. She held it tightly the whole way home.

The Next Day

Pa Lia's winter boots whispered as she walked into school. There was a hush in the hallways. Some of the kids were crying. Some of the teachers were crying, too.

Everything is different today. Pa Lia pulled off her hat and mittens. Calliope had called last night. She said Stinky Stern had died.

Pa Lia didn't tell Calliope she and Tou Ger had seen the accident. *I don't know if I can talk about it.*

Pa Lia put her backpack away. She walked into room 201 and gazed at their snowflakes on the wall.

"This is a very sad day," Mrs. Fennessey told the class. She had a tissue in her hand and a new box of tissues on her desk. "Most of you already know that Matthew Stern died last night. He was hit by a car yesterday after school. Some of you may have seen the accident."

14

Pa Lia held her breath. *Did Mrs. Fennessey see me there yesterday? Will she ask me to tell the class what I saw?*

"There will be an assembly this afternoon. Later a counselor will come to talk to our class about how we feel," said Mrs. Fennessey. "But for now, I think it would be good for *us* to talk about Matthew. To remember him. Perhaps some of you could help me."

Not me. Pa Lia took a breath. *Not yet. Maybe someone else will talk.*

Calliope raised her hand and shuffled up to the front of the room.

Thank you, Calliope.

"I went to preschool with Stinky. He had a stuffed hedgehog named Harold," said Calliope. "Harold came with Stinky every day. He had his own seat. His own cup."

Pa Lia picked up her pencil. She opened her spelling notebook. She found a clean page.

"Stinky really loved that hedgehog," said Calliope, and she scrambled back to her seat.

Pa Lia drew a tiny hedgehog. In tiny letters she wrote *Harold*.

A Place in the Choir

"Remember the bagpipes?" Howie blurted out.

Pa Lia looked up. Howie stood in front of the blackboard. Mrs. Fennessey didn't say, "Raise your hand first, Howie," or "Back to your seat right now, Howie."

Today *was* different.

Howie sighed. "I never really liked Stinky Stern," she said, "but it was special how he and his mom played those bagpipes in the Talent Show. Their music filled the whole gym. It was so beautiful."

Pa Lia felt like there was a huge storm inside her stomach. *I wish Stinky was still alive to play his bagpipes. I wish he could tell us why he sometimes did mean things and why he darted across the street yesterday.*

Howie wasn't done talking yet.

"Grandma Gardenia always sings a song about how all God's creatures got a place in the choir. It's about birds singing and stuff like that, but I think that it's about kids, too. Kids like Stinky." Howie glanced at Mrs. Fennessey. "I think Stinky Stern has a place in the choir."

Pa Lia closed her eyes. Thinking about Stinky singing like a bird somewhere calmed the swooshing and churning in her stomach.

She drew a Stinky Stern bird singing in a tree with lots of flowers around it. She put a shining, smiling sun in the sky.

Velvel

Oliver Hernandez moved so fast, Pa Lia almost didn't see him bolt by.

"Stinky's real name was Matthew Velvel Stern," said Oliver H. in a hurry. "He didn't want anyone at school to know that. He thought *Velvel* was a stupid name. He thought it sounded like *Velveeta*."

It sounds like velvet. Soft and beautiful. Pa Lia drew another bird, a bird with velvety wings.

"Matthew was my friend. I hope they write *Matthew Velvel Stern* on his gravestone. I think it was a good name. Better than *Stinky.*" Oliver H. flew back to his seat.

Matthew Velvel Stern, Pa Lia wrote. She drew curlicues and flowers around her his name. Her eyes felt hot and damp.

Pa Lia squinted to stop her tears. She saw a blurry Bridgett Thomas waiting to say something.

26

"One day just after my mom went back to work, my lunch fell in a puddle," said Bridgett. "I started to cry. Stinky said, 'Call your mommy, crybaby.' 'But my mommy's not home,' I told him."

Poor Bridgett.

Pa Lia's eyes filled with more tears.

Poor Stinky.

"'Oh, your mommy's not home? Your mommy must be on the moon,' Stinky said. 'I'm sending my mommy to the moon, too.' He zoomed and zoomed around me like he was a rocket ship. I stopped crying. Stinky made me laugh. He kept saying, 'One, two, three, blast off! To the moon, Mommy.'"

Stinky could be so silly, remembered Pa Lia. She fought hard not to think about what she had seen yesterday. She wrote *Blast off!* in balloon letters. *To the moon, Stinky Stern!*

Secret-Agent Man

Pa Lia pressed hard on her pencil. The point broke. She groped inside her desk for another pencil. One with a point.

"Ahem. Ahem. Ahem."

Madison Price was staring at her. She was trying to get Pa Lia to pay attention.

Does she think she is the teacher

today? Bossy show-off Madison. Pa Lia clutched her pencil and closed her desk. *Ready.*

"In kindergarten Stinky's dad walked him to school every day and waited until Stinky went inside," Madison told the class. She checked that Pa Lia was still listening. "All the kids called his dad secret-agent man. So one day Stinky and his dad wore huge rain-coats and sunglasses and big hats."

"I would have liked to see that," said Mrs. Fennessey.

Pa Lia drew a boy with a huge rain-coat and sunglasses and a big hat.

Madison finally sat down. A few kids raised their hands and told more Stinky stories. Molly Cohen told about her gold-fish, George Washington. He died while her family was on vacation.

"My mom flushed George down the toilet," said Molly. "I wish we had had a funeral for him."

Stinky thought toilets were very funny. Pa Lia drew a toilet.

But it wasn't funny without Stinky to make a joke about it.

"Will Stinky have a funeral? Can we go?" asked Molly.

"When I call the family later, I will find out," said Mrs. Fennessey.

A funeral. Stinky's funeral. Pa Lia chomped on her pencil. *Why didn't you look before you crossed the street?*

Vladmir Solbokin came in from ESL.

"I am sad today," he said.

Me, too, thought Pa Lia. She scribbled all over her toilet drawing. *Me, too.*

Will's Story

Pa Lia shuffled through the pages of her notebook. It was a loud shuffle. So loud she almost didn't hear Will Hobart. He was talking from his desk across the room.

"Stinky Stern was mean to me. He called me fatty pig face. He made me cry," began Will. He covered his eyes with his hands.

Pa Lia wanted to hug him. *Will is a very nice boy.*

"Stinky Stern is never coming back to school. He will never go to third grade with us. That is what it means to be dead. It means being gone. Always." Will put his head down on his desk.

Mrs. Fennessey put her hands on Will's shoulders.

Pa Lia shivered. *Stinky Stern is never coming back. Ever.*

"I know a lot of you are sad now. I am, too," said Mrs. Fennessey. "But you have shared some very important things today. You have helped me feel

closer to you and to Matthew. And I
thank you."

"It is almost time for lunch," she
said. "Is there anyone else who wants
to speak before we go?"

Pa Lia rubbed her
stomach. She looked
at the snowflakes on
the wall. *Yesterday
changed everything.*

Pa Lia hugged
herself. She shut
her eyes. She
could hear the
sirens blaring
again. She
could see the ambulance and its
flashing lights.

Stinky Stern is dead.

Gone.

Pa Lia put her pencil down. She closed her notebook. She raised her hand.

Mrs. Fennessey nodded.

Pa Lia took her snowflake off the wall. The glue still felt wet.

Stinky Stern Forever

Pa Lia stood by Stinky's desk. It was empty and clean.

"I was so mad at Stinky yesterday. He tried to ruin my snowflake. I was still mad at him when I saw the accident," Pa Lia began. She felt like a heavy bird had just flown from its nesting spot on her heart.

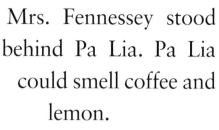

Mrs. Fennessey stood behind Pa Lia. Pa Lia could smell coffee and lemon.

"It happened so fast. I saw the white van hit Stinky," said Pa Lia. It was easier to talk now.

"*Stinky, get up. This is not funny,* I thought. But I knew he couldn't get up. And that was sadder and hurt more than anything Stinky ever said or did to me," said Pa Lia. Tears fell from behind her glasses.

"Stinky Stern is dead, but I will remember him forever. Stinky Stern forever," said Pa Lia. She let her snowflake fall gently on Stinky's desk.

Howie and Calliope took their snowflakes down. They put them next to Pa Lia's. They stood close to her.

"Stinky Stern forever," said Howie and Calliope.

All the kids in room 201 took their snowflakes off the wall.

"Stinky Stern forever," they said as they showered Stinky's desk with their snowflakes.

"Stinky Stern forever," said Mrs. Fennessey in a strong voice.

Today *was* different. No other day in room 201 would ever be like this one.

A Note from the Author

Stinky Stern Forever was a hard book for me to write. I had to dig deep inside myself to learn more about all of my characters. I had to understand what Stinky's death would mean to each of them. As I wrote, I would often find my hands getting cold and shaky. When I would pick up my youngest daughter at school, I would nervously watch the kids around me. *Would one of them dart into the street?*

It is very sad when someone you love dies. It is also sad when someone you don't love dies. Someone who has been mean to you. Someone like Matthew Velvel Stern. *Stinky Stern Forever* is a sad book, but it is a hopeful one, too, because Pa Lia and her classmates find their own special way to remember Stinky Stern—the good *and* the bad.

I know that when I write my next Jackson Friends book, I'm going to miss Matthew Stern a lot—even though he was a big-time stinker. But like the kids in Mrs. Fennessey's class, I have found my own way to remember him forever. I hope you will, too.

For reader's and teacher's guides to *Stinky Stern Forever* and to the other Jackson Friends books, visit the author's website at www.michelledwards.com.